The Adventures of Tom Sawyer

*Retold from the Mark Twain original
by Martin Woodside*

Illustrated by Lucy Corvino

Sterling Publishing Co., Inc.
New York

Library of Congress Cataloging-in-Publication Data
Woodside, Martin.
  The adventures of Tom Sawyer / abridged by Martin Woodside; illustrated
by Lucy Corvino; retold from the original author, Mark Twain.
      p. cm.—(Classic starts)
  Summary: An abridged version of the adventures of Tom and his friends
growing up in a small Missouri town on the banks of the Mississippi River in
the nineteenth century.
  ISBN 1-4027-1216-2
  [1. Mississippi—Fiction. 2. Missouri—History—19th century—Fiction. 3.
Adventure and adventurers—Fiction.] I. Title: Tom Sawyer. II. Corvino,
Lucy, ill. III. Twain, Mark, 1835–1910. Adventures of Tom Sawyer. IV. Title. V.
Series.
PZ7.W867Ad 2004
[Fic]—dc22
                                                          2004014500
                          6 8 10 9 7 5

Published by Sterling Publishing Co., Inc.
387 Park Avenue South, New York, NY 10016
Copyright © 2005 by Martin Woodside
Illustrations copyright © 2005 by Lucy Corvino
Distributed in Canada by Sterling Publishing
^c/o Canadian Manda Group, 165 Dufferin Street
Toronto, Ontario, Canada M6K 3H6
Distributed in the United Kingdom by GMC Distribution Services,
Castle Place, 166 High Street, Lewes, East Sussex, England BN7 1XU
Distributed in Australia by Capricorn Link (Australia) Pty. Ltd.
P.O. Box 704, Windsor, NSW 2756, Australia

Classic Starts is a trademark of Sterling Publishing Co., Inc.

Printed in China
All Rights Reserved
Design by Renato Stanisic

Sterling ISBN-13: 978-1-4027-1216-6
ISBN-10: 1-4027-1216-2

For information about custom editions, special sales, premium and
corporate purchases, please contact Sterling Special Sales
Department at 800-805-5489 or specialsales@sterlingpub.com.

CONTENTS

CHAPTER 1

Tom and the Fence

◦⌐◦

T om!"

No answer.

"TOM!"

No answer.

"Tom Sawyer, you come on out here!"

Aunt Polly scrunched her eyes and carefully looked over the bedroom. She'd turned the house upside down but there was still no sign of the adventurous boy. "You just wait until I get ahold of you!" Tom's aunt muttered as she poked under the bed with the broom without success.

Seeing an open window, she stuck her head out, scanning the garden for a glimpse of her headstrong nephew, but all she saw there was the stack of wood he hadn't cut and the grass he hadn't mowed. Suddenly hearing a small squeak behind her, she turned just in time to seize the small boy by his collar.

"Aha!" she cried in triumph. "I knew I should have checked that closet right off! Now, what's that on your mouth?"

Tom Sawyer stood before his aunt with his lips smeared a bright red.

"Nothing, ma'am."

"Nothing indeed! Why that's the fresh raspberry jam I made for Mrs. Harper! And what's that? Take your hands out of those pockets."

As Tom slowly took his hands out, a white powder trail began raining down onto the floor.

Aunt Polly shoved her hands into the pockets of Tom's overalls. "My goodness!" she cried in disbelief, "you must have a pound of sugar in there!" She put her hands on her hips and looked down at her nephew: "Tom Sawyer, that is absolutely the last straw!"

The very next day was Saturday, and a fine summer Saturday it was. The morning sky was bright and fresh and the whole world brimmed with life. Tom, however, stood sadly out on the sidewalk with a bucket of whitewash and a long-handled brush. He looked at the fence in front of Aunt Polly's house. It was at least nine feet high and ran nearly half the block long, and Tom had to paint it all as punishment for the mischief he had caused the day before. Sighing loudly, he dipped the brush in the bucket and began daubing one of the fence boards.

After only a few strokes, Tom sat down. He began to think of all the fun he'd planned for the day. It was such a fine day for fishing, for fighting, for all kinds of adventuring, but Tom knew that painting the fence would take up all afternoon. Worse, other boys would come by soon and see him doing his chores while they had the whole day free for *their* adventures. Tom could barely stand the thought of it. Slowly, he got up and started back to work, dipping the brush into the bucket of whitewash and making long strokes over the boards of the fence.

Tom hadn't been at work five minutes when he heard a sound he feared. It was whistling and not just any whistling; it was the whistling of a boy set out on some great quest. Tom turned his head halfway and saw Ben Rogers bounding down the street with a hop-skip-and-a-jump, a shiny green apple in his hand.

Tom turned back to his painting, but just then he had an idea. He stood up straight and stared at the fence in front of him with deep concentration. Curious at what Tom was doing, Ben Rogers now stopped right behind the silent boy. Tom could still hear him whistling. There was a pause, and then the sound of a big juicy crunch as Ben took a bite out of his apple. Pretending that he hadn't seen Ben at all, Tom started painting again.

Ben Rogers started whistling again, this time even louder, but Tom kept on painting.

"Got to work, hey?" Ben finally snickered.

Tom didn't turn around to answer. Instead, he put his brush down and crossed his arms. He then rubbed his chin with one hand and stared at the fence as if he were working out some great mystery.

"I say." Ben coughed in yet another attempt to get Tom's attention. "Aunt Polly put you to work?"

Tom turned suddenly as if shocked to see someone there.

"Gosh, Ben! I didn't know you was there."

"I'll bet you didn't." Ben smiled before taking another bite out of his delicious apple. "I'm going to the swimming hole. Don't you wish you could come along? Of course, I'm sure you'd rather work all day."

Tom looked Ben over slowly, from head to toe. With a puzzled face, he asked, "What work are you talking about?"

"Ain't *that* work," Ben said, pointing at the paintbrush and the fence.

Tom looked Ben over again. Then he turned around, picked up his brush, and resumed painting.

"I suppose you're going to tell me you *like* painting that fence," Ben called out.

Tom didn't turn around but simply said, "It's not every day a boy gets to paint a whole fence by himself."

Ben stopped in midbite and watched Tom run the brush daintily over the wood fence, stepping back every stroke or two to admire his work.

"Say, Tom, let *me* try."

Tom stopped. He slowly turned to Ben while pretending to consider his idea for a moment.

"No, no, I'm sorry. Aunt Polly wouldn't like that. She said there ain't one boy in a thousand that's fit to paint this fence."

"Come on, Tom," Ben moaned. "Let me just try. Please. Just one stroke. I'd let *you*, if you was me."

Tom started rubbing his chin again, looking Ben over just as seriously as he'd been looking that fence over.

"I'll give you my apple!" Ben cried out.

Tom considered a moment longer. Then, very slowly, he handed the brush over to Ben Rogers.

Sitting under a shady tree, Tom—now no longer gloomy—savored the last tasty bite of the green apple and watched Ben paint the fence in the hot sun. Tom thought he had discovered something wonderful. To make a boy want something, all you had to do was make that something hard to get!

CHAPTER 2

Showing Off in Sunday School

⤳

At breakfast the next day, Tom was still in a happy mood. With his belly full of ample portions of Aunt Polly's delicious hotcakes, he couldn't help but reflect on his success with Ben Rogers the day before. Suddenly, Tom remembered that it was Sunday, and Sunday meant much more than a great breakfast. As Aunt Polly got out her gold leaf Bible and announced that it was time for family worship, Tom let out a mournful groan.

An agonizing half an hour later, the boy was

excused to memorize his verses for Sunday school.

"I done mine yesterday," his brother Sid said. Grinning from ear to ear, Sid then raced out the front door to go play.

"Quit fooling around, Tom!" Aunt Polly called. "Your cousin Mary will be here any minute now."

Tom trudged off to his room and blew the dust off his tiny Bible. He had five Bible verses to memorize. Tom picked the Sermon on the Mount on account of those being the five shortest verses he could find. An hour later he woke up, facedown in the holy book, with his cousin Mary's voice ringing in his ear.

"Hard at work I see." Mary's eyes danced brightly as she took the book from her cousin. "Let me hear you recite."

Tom bent all his energies to remembering what he hadn't read.

"Blessed are the a—a—"

"Poor," Mary prompted.

"Yes—poor. Blessed are the poor—i—i"

"In spirit." And on it went, with Tom stuttering through the verses and Mary reminding him gently. After a slow and painful hour, Mary announced it was now time for Tom to get dressed for Sunday school.

After another groan from the boy—this one even louder than the one before—Mary helped Tom into his Sunday suit, buttoning his shirt to the top and fastening his necktie tightly. Tom made a face, feeling every bit as uncomfortable as he looked, as Mary brushed him off and crowned him with a speckled straw hat. He growled at Sid, who had come in from playing and was laughing at his brother from the doorway. Although he tried, Tom couldn't think of anything he hated more than Sunday school.

Unlike Tom, his cousin Mary loved going to

Sunday school, and she had even won some prizes there. If you could recite two verses from the Bible, you got a blue ticket from the Sunday school teacher, a tall, slim man with blond hair and a deep booming voice named Walters. Ten blue tickets were equal to a red ticket, and ten red tickets were equal to a yellow one. For ten yellow tickets, you could become the proud owner of a plainly bound Bible. Two thousand verses seemed to Tom a heavy price to pay for such a prize. But Mary had won two of the Bibles, and a German-born boy had laid claim to four or five! Although Tom had no use for such a prize, he still longed for the glory that came with earning it. After all, the delivery of the Bibles was a rare and noteworthy event.

The sun shone brightly as Tom slowly walked behind Mary and Sid down the dusty road to Sunday school. At the door of the church, Tom saw Billy, another friend of his who had also been dragged kicking and screaming into his Sunday best. Suddenly, Tom got an idea.

"Say, Billy, you got a yeller ticket?"

"Yes."

"What'll you take for her?"

"What'll you give?"

"Piece of lickerish and a fishhook."

"Let's see 'em."

The goods were examined, and the deal was done. Tom had a pile of such treasure in his pockets, and before too long, he had traded all of it for tickets: yellow, red, even blue tickets. When the bell finally rang for church, Tom's pockets were stuffed with tickets.

Mr. Walters' Sunday school class was a restless, noisy, troublesome bunch of children, and Tom was the worst of them all. He couldn't resist pulling the hair of the first boy he saw even though Mr. Walters immediately scolded him. But as soon as Mr. Walters turned his back, Tom poked the boy in front of him with a pin.

"Ouch!" yelped the boy, and Mr. Walters was yelling at Tom again.

Eventually, both Tom and the class settled down, and Mr. Walters listened patiently as the children stumbled through their verses. Finally, after everyone had finished reciting, Mr. Walters spoke. "Now children," he announced, "I want you all to sit up as straight and pretty as you can and give me all of your attention."

As much as he tried to listen to what his Sunday school teacher was saying about a new family in town, Tom still felt his eyelids growing heavy. When they finally fluttered open, he saw that everyone was staring toward the back of the classroom at a chubby, middle-aged man with dark hair and spectacles and a very well-dressed and dignified lady. Although both the man and woman were quite grand looking, it was the sight of their young daughter that caught Tom's eye.

She was a lovely girl with blue eyes and blond hair plaited into two long tails. As soon as he saw her face, Tom began making mischief again, pulling hair, making faces—in short, doing everything he could think of to try to gain her attention.

After Mr. Walters had settled the class down again, he introduced the visitors and seated them in the front of the room. The chubby man turned out to be Judge Thatcher, the greatest judge in the county, and his daughter was named Becky. Now, thanks in part to Tom, everyone else began showing off. Mr. Walters loudly shouted out instructions while tending to pupils who were struggling with their reading and wagging fingers at those who were misbehaving. The students scrapped and scuffled and some filled the air with wads of paper. All the while, the great Judge Thatcher beamed a majestic smile as he presided over the noisy class.

For Mr. Walters, there was only one thing missing from the scene: the chance to deliver a Bible prize and exhibit one of his best young students to Judge Thatcher. He'd checked with all his star pupils, but no one had more than a few yellow tickets. Mr. Walters had just about given up hope when—of all people!—Tom Sawyer came forward holding in his hand nine yellow, nine red, and ten blue tickets. Tom's teacher turned pale; he hadn't expected to see anything like this for another ten years at least. Shaking his head in disbelief, he counted the tickets once, twice, and then a third time while Tom grinned from ear to ear.

And just like that, Tom Sawyer now became the envy of the whole class. The other students stared at him with bitter jealousy, especially those who now knew too late what they'd done by trading those tickets. Tom couldn't resist basking in the glory of the moment as Mr. Walters shook his hand vigorously.

Becky Thatcher looked at Tom with some interest, but Tom didn't dare look in her direction; he couldn't bear to. When he was introduced to Judge Thatcher, he became so nervous that his tongue was tied and his heart started pounding. The judge put his hand on Tom's head, gently ruffling his hair, and asked him what his name was.

"T-Tom. Thomas."

"Tell the gentleman your other name," Mr. Walters urged, starting to get more than a bit nervous himself. "And don't forget your manners."

"Thomas Sawyer—sir."

"That's it! That's a good boy," exclaimed the judge. "And two thousand verses! That's a great, great many. Knowledge is what makes great men and good men. You will be a great man, Thomas, and one day you'll say, 'It's all owing to the precious Sunday school privileges of my boyhood.' You'll be glad you spent the time to learn those two thousand verses. You won't regret it at all. Now," and the great man eagerly put his hands together, "you wouldn't mind sharing some of that knowledge with me, would you? No doubt, you know the names of all twelve disciples. Would you mind telling us the names of two of them?"

Mr. Walters tugged at his collar. He was starting to sweat, and he stared at Tom, who was now silent and blushing. "Is it possible," Tom's teacher thought to himself, "is it really possible the boy cannot answer the simplest question?"

Poor Tom was tugging at his buttonhole as his

mind raced wildly, hoping desperately that he would somehow recall the right names.

"Answer the gentleman," Mr. Walters said hopefully. "Don't be afraid."

"Now, come along, Thomas," the judge urged, this time a bit more sternly. "The names of the first two disciples were—"

"DAVID AND GOLIATH!"

And then Tom ran out of the room as the rest of his Sunday school classmates howled with laughter.

CHAPTER 3

Tom Meets Becky

Monday morning always made Tom miserable. With it began another week's slow suffering in school. Up early, Tom sat in bed thinking about the evils of school and how he could be free of them. He felt his head, hoping it was warm. Sadly, it wasn't. He inspected his body, hoping to find symptoms of some terrible illness. There were none. Just knowing that he was healthy made him feel even worse than before.

Soon Tom was on the way to class feeling, as

usual, in very low spirits when he came upon Huckleberry Finn.

Huck Finn, the son of a local troublemaker, was hated and dreaded by all the mothers in town but loved and envied by their children. He came and went at his own free will and never had to go to church or school. Huck could go fishing or swimming whenever he chose and even stay up nights as late at he pleased. He was really great at swearing and Tom Sawyer, like every other boy, was strictly forbidden to play with him. So, not surprisingly, Tom played with Huck Finn whenever he got the chance.

"Hello there, Huckleberry!"

"Hello yourself, Tom."

"What's that you got inside that pouch?"

"A medicine potion."

"My, it smells awful. What's in it?"

"Catfish whiskers, four-leaf clovers, owl eggs, and other stuff."

"What other stuff?"

"That's none of your business."

"What it's good for, Huck?"

"Good for? It cures warts if you use it right!"

"How do you cure warts with it?"

"Well, that's easy. You take the potion to the graveyard at midnight. That's when a devil will come, maybe two or three; they come to get someone wicked who's died. And when they're taking that feller away, you throw the pouch with the potion in it after 'em. Then you say, 'Devil follow corpse, potion follow devil, warts follow potion! No more warts.'"

"Did you ever try it, Huck?"

"Nope."

"When do you think you're going to?"

"Tonight. I reckon those devils ought to be there to get old Hoss Williams."

"But they buried him Saturday. Didn't they get him that night?"

"Why, how you talk! How could they come till midnight?—and *then* it's Sunday. Devils don't slosh around much on Sunday, I don't reckon."

"I never thought of that. Let me go with you," Tom pleaded.

"Of course," Huck replied. "That is," Huck stared at him, "assuming you ain't too afraid."

"Not likely!" Tom shot back. Then, real quiet-like, he whispered to Huck, "Will you also tell me the other ingredients in the potion?"

"I will—if you show you me that you ain't afraid."

"I'm not afraid of anything, Huck Finn."

"We'll see about that."

"I reckon we will."

The two boys went on talking like this for some time before Tom remembered he had to go to school. Before leaving, he reminded Huckleberry Finn one more time not to forget to come fetch him that very night.

When Tom finally entered the classroom, his schoolmaster, Mr. Dobbins, was quietly dozing in the front of the room, so Tom threw himself into his seat hoping no one would notice.

No such luck.

"Thomas Sawyer!"

Whenever he heard his full name pronounced, Tom knew it meant trouble.

"Come up here, Thomas. Now sir, suppose you tell us why you were late once again."

Tom had been thinking up a lie—a good lie, a doozy of a lie—as he walked slowly to the front of the room. Then he saw those two long tails of yellow hair hanging down and recognized the Thatcher girl sitting all the way on the girls' side of the schoolroom right next to an empty seat. Quick as a wink, he knew what he had to say next.

"I stopped to talk to Huckleberry Finn!" Tom said loudly.

All eyes were on Tom Sawyer now, and his

classmates wondered if he'd lost his mind.

"What did you say?" Mr. Dobbins asked, not believing his own ears.

"I stopped to talk to Huckleberry Finn." Tom spoke slowly, so there was no mistaking the words.

"Thomas Sawyer, that is the most amazing confession I have ever heard. Take off your jacket, sir!"

Dobbins got out his switch, and Tom stuck his arm out bravely to accept his punishment.

Several loud whacks soon filled the air, and Tom winced with each one. Finally, the schoolmaster got tired and he put his switch down.

"Now sir," he said sternly, "go and sit with the *girls*! And let that be a warning to you."

Tom took a seat at the end of the pine bench next to the girl with the long blond tails. Nudges, winks, and whispers soon ran from one end of the room to another. Meanwhile, Tom sat perfectly still, his arms perched on the long, low desk, and seemed to study his book. Although he wore a blank look on his face, inside he couldn't have been happier.

Eventually, the students turned back to their work, and the schoolmaster got back to dozing. Seizing his chance, Tom stole a glance at the beautiful girl beside him, but Becky only made a face at Tom before turning her head away. When, cautiously, she turned back, she saw a fresh peach on her desk. She quickly pushed it away. Tom gently put it back. She thrust the peach away again, and again Tom returned it, gently. This time she let it sit while Tom wrote on his paper: "Please take it— I got more." Becky read the message but said nothing. Now Tom began drawing something else on his paper, hiding his work with his left arm. Becky pretended not to notice what Tom was writing, but her curiosity soon got the better of her. She strained to see it, but Tom acted as if he didn't notice her at all. "Let me look at it," Becky finally whispered.

Tom half uncovered the drawing—a crude house with a swirl of smoke floating up from the chimney.

"It's peachy. Can you make a man?"

So Tom drew a man standing in the front yard. He was big enough to step over the house without much trouble, but the girl didn't mention this.

"He's dandy. Now can you draw a girl like me coming along?"

Tom drew an hourglass

with a full moon for a head and straw limbs for arms.

"It's ever so nice," Becky said. "I wish I could draw."

"It's easy," Tom whispered. "I'll learn you."

"Oh, will you? When?"

"At noon. Do you go home for lunch?"

"I'll stay if you want me to, Thomas Sawyer."

"That's only my name when I'm in trouble. Call me Tom, won't you?"

"Yes."

Tom smiled, then fell to working again, covering his paper with his hand. He wrote something there but he kept it covered up. Again, Becky pleaded with Tom to see it.

"Oh, it ain't nothing," Tom mumbled.

"Yes it is."

"You wouldn't want to see it."

"Yes, I do want to see it. Please let me."

"Are you sure?"

"I am."

"Oh, *you* don't want to see," Tom said coyly.

With this reply, a small scuffle ensued. Becky put her hand over Tom's paper and tried to pull it from him. Tom pretended to resist, but he finally let her drag his hand away. Revealed on the paper were the following words: *"I love you."*

"Oh, you bad thing!" Becky said as she slapped him sharply on the hand.

Still, Tom could tell from her face that she was pleased.

But at just this very moment, Tom suddenly felt a tight grip locking around his ear. The next thing he knew, he was being lifted out of his seat by his ear by Mr. Dobbins, who dragged him clear across the room before rudely dumping him back again into his regular seat in the boys' section. Meanwhile, the whole schoolroom burst into fits of wild giggles at the sight. But although Tom's ears tingled, his heart was filled with joy.

CHAPTER 4

Heartbreak Comes Quickly

Outside, the sun shone and the air smelled fresh, but inside the classroom not a breath of air was stirring. As Tom watched two bluebirds float lazily through the clear cloud-free sky, he felt that recess would never come. He looked at Becky, who was busy with her studies, and thought that she was even prettier than Amy Lawrence, whom he had first courted in school. When noon finally came, the students quickly poured out through the doors of the schoolhouse to race home for lunch. As Becky got up from her seat, Tom whispered in her ear:

"Go on out with the rest of 'em. When you get to the corner, give 'em the slip, turn through the lane, and come back. I'll meet up with you."

Soon enough, the two classmates were back at the now empty school. They sat together with a blank page before them. Tom handed Becky his pencil. He held her hand, guiding it, and a short while later, another house appeared on the page. Becky smiled up at him.

"Do you like rats?" Tom asked, after their interest in art had faded.

"No, I hate them!"

"Well I hate them, too—*live* ones. But I'm talking about dead ones."

"No, I don't care for rats. What *I like* is chewing gum."

"Oh, I should say so. I wish I had some now."

"I've got some."

So Tom and Becky sat quietly and chewed

gum for a while, dangling their legs against the bench.

"Was you ever at a circus?" Tom asked.

"Yes, and my pa promised to take me again if I'm good."

"I been to the circus three or four times. I'm going to be a clown in the circus when I grow up."

"Oh, that'll be nice. They're so lovely, all spotted up and such."

"And they get buckets of money—I hear even a dollar a day."

Tom then took a deep breath—

"Say, Becky, was you ever engaged?"

"No."

"Would you like to?"

"I don't know. What's it like?"

"Like? Why, it ain't like anything. You just tell a boy you won't have anyone but him, ever ever *ever,* and then you kiss and that's all. Anyone can do it."

"What do you kiss for?"

"Well, that's what everyone does. You remember what I wrote down on the paper for you?"

"Yes."

"What was it?"

"I won't tell you."

"I'll tell you," Tom said, and he reached over and put his arm around Becky's waist and whispered *"I love you"* into her ear.

"Now you whisper it to me—just the same way."

Becky hesitated for a moment. Tom turned his face away and she bent over timidly, whispering faintly in his ear:

"I—love—you."

Then she sprang up and ran around the desks and benches and into a corner of the room, where she hid her face behind her arms.

"Now, Becky," Tom said, trying to comfort

her, "it's all over. All over but the kiss—and you mustn't be afraid of that."

Becky stayed that way, her back to him in the corner, face buried in her arms for a while. Tom kept talking, trying to convince her of the virtues of a kiss, until finally she turned and let her arms drop. Tom kissed her gently.

"Now it's done. You ain't ever to love anyone but me, Becky, and you ain't ever to marry anyone else, either."

"I'll never love anyone else, Tom, and you ain't ever to, either."

"Of course not. That's a part of it. When we walk to school or play at parties, we'll always be together."

"It's so nice. I never heard of it before."

"It's wonderful! Why, me and Amy Lawrence—"

And Tom stopped, realizing his mistake instantly.

"Oh, Tom. I-I'm not the first you been engaged to."

Becky began to cry.

"No, Becky, no," Tom pleaded. "Don't cry. I don't care for Amy anymore."

But Becky kept on crying. Tom tried to put his arm around her neck but she pushed him away. Watching Becky cry made his heart ache. He stood there uneasily, not sure what to do or say.

"Becky, I-I don't care for anybody but you."

Still no reply. Just sobs.

"Becky, won't you say something?"

More sobs. Tom searched his pockets and took out his most prized possession—a shiny brass star from the top of a fence.

"Please, Becky, won't you take it?"

She knocked the treasure to the floor.

That was it for Tom.

Now feeling angry as well as sad, Tom marched out of the schoolhouse and began running. He ran on and on past Cardiff Hill and behind the Douglas Mansion. He kept on running until the schoolhouse was barely visible. Then he sat down for a long time with his elbows on his knees and his chin in his hands. What had he done? Tom thought. He had meant the best in the world and been treated like a dog—a dog! What if he turned his back now and disappeared completely? Becky would be sorry then!

Then Tom had an idea. He would become a pirate, an adventure he had long dreamed about. How great it would be to go sail the dancing seas in a sleek black ship with a pirate flag tied to the mast. And after he became famous for his brave deeds, he would return to his old sleepy town of St. Petersburg, Missouri, and march into the church with his tall black boots and his red sash, his pistols and sword tucked into his belt. Everyone, even Becky, would then look at him and whisper, "It's Tom Sawyer the Famous Pirate!—the bravest man who ever sailed a ship!"

His future decided, Tom jumped to his feet and ran through the forest, imagining his wonderful new life on the high seas.

CHAPTER 5

Tragedy in the Graveyard

∽

Tom's pirate adventures would have to wait for a while since he had to meet up with Huck Finn that very night. After it got dark, Tom did his best to lie still in his bed, so as not to wake his brother Sid and arouse his suspicions. But Tom's eyes stayed wide open, staring at the dark window. The night was quiet, but Tom could hear every-thing—from the creaking of the wood rafters to the crickets chirping outside. Then, suddenly, a dog barked in the distance. It was soon followed by a loud crash, the sound of glass breaking against Aunt Polly's woodshed, and a voice crying out:

"Scat, you devil!"

A minute later, Tom was dressed and headed out the window, down to the garden where Huck Finn was waiting. A half hour later, the boys were creeping through the tall grass of the graveyard.

The graveyard sat perched on a hill and was surrounded by an old, crumbling fence that leaned inward in some places, outward in others, and went every direction but straight. All the graves were covered with weeds and dead grass. A faint wind moaned through the branches of the trees. Tom felt sure it was the voices of the dead, upset at being disturbed. The two boys stepped carefully, making their way to the heap of new stones that marked Hoss Williams' grave. There were three great elms bunched together near the grave, and the boys settled in behind them.

For a long time nothing happened. As the

silence grew deep, Tom became more and more fearful.

"It's awful quiet, Tom," said Huck Finn.

"Too quiet."

There was a long pause. Finally, Tom whispered again:

"Say, Huck, do you think Hoss Williams can hear us talking?"

"Of course he can," Huck said. "At least, his spirit can."

The conversation died again; Tom didn't dare to speak, wondering whether or not Hoss Williams's ghost was listening and if he thought badly of them. Suddenly, he shot up, grabbing Huck's arm.

"Sh!"

"What is it, Tom?"

The boys clung together, two hearts beating wildly.

"*Sh*! There it is again!"

"Tom, they're coming. The devils're coming for sure. What do we do?"

"I dunno. Will they see us?"

"Oh, Tom, they can see in the dark, just like cats. Why did we come here?"

"Don't be afraid, Huck. If we keep perfectly still, maybe they won't notice us at all."

The boys sat silently, scarcely daring to breathe. Three strange figures approached, one of them swinging an old-fashioned tin lantern that freckled the ground with light.

"It's devils fer sure," Huck whispered. "We're done for!"

Tom started praying:

"Now I lay me down to sleep—"

"*Sh!*"

"What is it, Huck?"

"That's Muff Potter's voice. They're human!"

"It can't be."

"But it is. Keep still. He's too busy to notice us."

"Say, Huck, I know another one of those voices. It's Injun Joe!"

The boys grew quiet again as the mysterious visitors had reached the grave and now stood just a few feet from the trees that Tom and Huck were hiding behind.

"Here it is," said the third voice, holding up his lantern to reveal young Dr. Robinson.

Muff Potter and Injun Joe were carrying a wheelbarrow with a couple of shovels and some rope in it. Dropping their load, they began to open Hoss Williams' grave. The doctor placed the lantern at the head of the grave, and then sat back against one of the elm trees, so close that the boys could have touched him.

"Hurry up," he said in a low voice. "The moon will be out soon."

The two other men growled and kept on with their digging. Tom and Huck listened to the noisy sound of the spades hitting dirt and gravel.

In barely a whisper, Tom asked Huck, "What are they doing?"

"G-grave robbing," Huck replied in a faint, trembling voice. "Doctors sometimes use dead bodies for experiments and stuff, but they ain't supposed to."

Finally, the boys heard a different sound as one of the shovels struck the wooden coffin. Muff Porter and Injun Joe then used the rope to pull the coffin up as Dr. Robinson sat and watched. They pulled up the lid and rudely dumped the body out onto the ground. The moon was out now. Rising through the clouds, it cast a glow on Hoss Williams' pale, lifeless face. Then Williams was lifted into the wheelbarrow, and Injun Joe covered him with a blanket while Muff Potter firmly tied down the body then cut off rope with his knife.

"The darn thing's done," Injun Joe said. "Now, it'll be five dollars more if you want it to go anywhere."

"What's the meaning of this?" Dr. Robinson said, jumping to his feet. "We agreed on a price and you were paid in advance."

"That's not all you done," Injun Joe growled, stepping closer. "Five years ago I came to your father's kitchen, begging for something to eat. Your father had me jailed as a drifter. Did you forget? Did you think I'd forget?"

Injun Joe was closer now, shaking his fist in the doctor's face. Suddenly, Robinson punched Injun Joe, hitting him so hard that he fell flat on his back.

"Say," Muff Potter cried angrily, dropping his knife, "don't hit my partner!"

Potter then started fighting with the doctor. As they struggled, Injun Joe got back to his feet. Snatching up Potter's knife, he crept carefully behind the doctor. All at once, the doctor pushed Potter away and grabbed the heavy headboard from Hoss Williams' grave. He swung it hard and knocked out Muff Potter with one blow. In the same instant, Injun Joe saw his chance and drove the knife into the doctor's chest.

"Injun Joe *always* settles his scores."

Then he robbed the doctor's body, taking his watch and wallet. Next, Injun Joe took the bloody knife and placed it in Muff Potter's hand. Then he sat down on the empty coffin and waited.

Soon enough, Muff Potter moaned, closing his hand on the knife. His eyes opened, and the sight of the blade in his hand sent a shudder straight through him.

"Joe." He sat up, looking at his partner confusedly. "Joe, what happened?"

"It's dirty business," Injun Joe answered. "What did you do it for?"

"I-I didn't, Joe."

"Stop it now. That talk won't wash."

Potter trembled and grew white.

"Joe. I-I can't remember a thing. It's them dizzy spells. It's awful Joe, just awful. He was so young!"

"You two was scuffling," Injun Joe said calmly. "He hit you with that headboard and laid you out. You surprised him. You grabbed that knife and jammed it into him just as he hit you again."

"It's these spells that done it," Muff moaned. "I never used a weapon in my life." The poor fellow dropped to his knees, clasping his hands. "Say you won't tell, Joe. Please, I beg of you."

"You've always been square with me," Joe replied. "No, I won't tell."

"Oh, Joe, I'll bless you for this as long as you live." And with that Muff Potter started to cry.

"There's no time for that," Injun Joe said, shaking his partner by the shoulders. "You need to move now, far away, and don't leave no tracks behind you."

Muff slowly got to his feet. "Thank you, Joe," he said. "Oh, thank you."

Injun Joe smiled wickedly as he watched Muff Potter start to run away.

The moon now passed behind a cloud. Coming out again, it shone on the murdered doctor, the blanketed corpse, the lidless coffin, and the open grave. All was still again.

Tom and Huck were speechless with horror as they fled the scene. They feared they were followed but didn't dare look back as they raced through the trees and past the cottages out by the edge of the village. The old tannery lay ahead, and both boys fixed their eyes on it.

"I can't stand it much longer," Tom whispered hoarsely.

Huck was panting too hard to respond. The tannery got closer and closer until they finally burst through its open door. Shutting it behind them, the boys collapsed on the floor. For a while, the only sound to be heard was that of their own heavy breathing.

"Huckleberry, what do you reckon'll come of this?"

"Hanging. If Dr. Robinson's dead, it means hanging."

Tom thought a while.

"But who'll tell?' He thought again. "Will *we* tell, Huck?"

"What are you talking about? Suppose something happens and Injun Joe escapes hanging. He'd come after us for sure. Let Muff Potter tell."

"Huck, Muff Potter *can't* tell because he doesn't know. He was out cold the whole time!"

"By golly, that's so!"

There was another long pause.

"Huck, you reckon you can keep quiet?"

"Tom, we've *got* to keep quiet. Injun Joe wouldn't think twice about stabbing us. We've got to swear it, Tom, swear to keep mum."

"It's the best thing. We'll just shake hands and swear that we——"

"No, Tom, that won't do. That'll do for little things—with gals and stuff—but this is serious. We need to have writing. And blood."

Tom picked up a clean shingle that lay in the moonlight and took a little piece of red chalk that lay in his pocket. Working slowly, he scrawled out the following lines:

Huck Finn and Tom Sawyer Swears they will keep Mum about this and they wish they may drop down Dead if they ever Tell.

Next, Tom took a needle from his pocket and each boy pricked his thumb, squeezing out a drop of blood. Tom signed his initials, using the ball of his little finger, and then showed Huck, who never learned to write, how to make an "H" and an "F."

"Tom, does that keep us from *ever* telling?"

"I reckon so."

By the time Tom finally crept back through his bedroom window, the night was nearly over. He took off his clothes slowly and eased quietly into bed so as not to wake up his brother. What Tom didn't know was that it was Sid who was now pretending to be asleep. When Tom woke up, Sid was dressed and gone. Why hadn't Aunt Polly come to wake him? Tom wondered. Downstairs, the family had finished breakfast. Tom felt sore and drowsy and the silence at the table chilled him. No one even looked him in the eye.

When Aunt Polly finally spoke to him, she began weeping and asking him how he could keep breaking her old heart so. Hearing her cry, Tom's heart grew as sore as his tired body. He cried and pleaded with her for forgiveness, and he promised to be good over and over again. He felt so bad that he even forgot to be angry with Sid for telling on him. Aunt Polly, however, said nothing. Now grief stricken, Tom moped off to school.

CHAPTER 6

Tom Wrestles with His Conscience

By lunchtime, news about Dr. Robinson's grisly murder had spread through the whole town. Mr. Dobbins dismissed class for the rest of the day because no one could think about anything else but the gruesome event the night before.

Muff Potter's bloody knife had been found close to Robinson's body, and someone had seen Potter washing in the creek at about two o'clock in the morning. The talk was that the town was being turned upside down to find the "murderer."

Slowly, many of the townspeople began

drifting to the graveyard, and Tom decided to join the procession. Arriving at the dreadful place, he wormed his way to the front of the crowd. Huckleberry Finn soon pushed his way up to Tom's side.

"Poor fellow, poor young fellow!" someone offered.

"This oughta be a lesson for grave robbers," another chimed in.

Tom looked across the crowd, and his heart nearly stopped when he saw the stony face of Injun Joe. At this moment, a murmur went through the crowd.

"There he is!" a voice shouted. "There's Muff Potter!"

"Don't let him get away!"

Muff Potter just stood there looking confused. When he saw the murdered man, poor Muff started shaking violently.

"I didn't do it, friends," he sobbed. "I swear on my honor I never done it."

"Is that not your knife?" the sheriff asked, shoving the blade in front of Potter's face.

Muff would have collapsed just then, but some men close by caught him and eased him to the ground. Muff sat there sobbing until he spotted Injun Joe, and his face lit up.

"Tell 'em, Joe, tell'em! It ain't no use holding back now."

Tom and Huck stood silent and held their breath as they stared at Injun Joe, waiting for him to speak. Calm as he could be, Joe reeled off a tale full of lies. He told how Potter had struggled with Dr. Robinson and then how he'd killed him.

"Why didn't you leave?" someone asked, turning back to Muff. "What did you come back here for?"

"I-I couldn't help it," Potter moaned. "I

wanted to run away, but I couldn't come anywhere but here."

Muff Potter fell to crying again while Injun Joe repeated his story, this time under oath. The boys were stunned both by Injun Joe's lies and by the fact that they'd gone unpunished. But both Tom and Huck were too afraid to tell the truth for fear of Injun Joe's revenge.

To make matters even worse, Becky Thatcher had fallen ill and had stopped coming to school. What if she should die! Tom worried so much that he found that he could no longer take an interest in much of anything, not even in becoming a pirate. Every day, he reached school ahead of time. Rather than playing with his friends, he hung about by the school's front gate, his gaze fixed down the road.

A group of girls came into view, and Tom hated each and every one of them for being the wrong one. Giving up hope, he turned to go into the dreary schoolhouse. Just then, another girl appeared in the distance. The next instant Tom was yelling, laughing, and chasing the other boys around. He jumped over the fence—at risk of life and limb—threw handsprings, and stood on his head. Tom did these heroic things all the while keeping a close eye on Becky. Next, he started war whooping, snatched a boy's cap and threw it onto the roof of the schoolhouse, and broke through a group of boys, tumbling them to the ground before he sprawled out directly in front of Becky—nearly knocking her over.

"Hm̀m!" Becky turned with her nose up in the air. "Some people think they're smart— always showing off!"

Tom's cheeks burned. He picked himself up and sneaked off, feeling crushed.

At lunch that day, Tom ignored Becky

completely. He pretended not to see her tripping happily back and forth, her face flushed, playing with the other classmates and obviously trying to get his attention. He even went so far as to strike up a conversation with Amy Lawrence.

At recess, Tom continued to flirt with Amy, doing everything he could to make sure that Becky saw him. But when he finally found her, Becky was sitting cozily on a little bench behind the schoolhouse, looking at a picture book with Alfred Temple. So absorbed were they, so close together were their little heads over the book, that they didn't seem aware of anything else in the whole world, least of all Tom and Amy.

Jealousy now ran red-hot through Tom's veins. Unable to bear the sight of Becky and Alfred a moment longer, Tom said good-bye to Amy and raced home. Becky went right on look-ing at pictures with Alfred, but with no Tom there to suffer, the minutes began to drag, and she grew sad. Seeing that he was losing her, Alfred kept exclaiming:

"Oh, here's a jolly one. Look at this!"

"Oh, don't bother me! I don't care for them!" Becky cried. Then she burst into tears and walked away.

CHAPTER 7

Brave Tom

꩜

At recess time, Tom liked nothing better than to head home for one of Aunt Polly's tasty lunches. Today, however, he barely touched his food. Finally, Tom decided once and for all to make things right with Becky, and he felt his spirits began to lift. A half hour later, he was headed back to school when he came across Becky walking down Meadow Lane. Without a moment's hesitation, he ran over to her.

"I acted mighty mean today, Becky, and I'm so

sorry. I won't ever, ever act that way again as long as I ever live. Please, make up with me, won't you?"

The girl stopped and looked at him with her eyes full of scorn.

"I'll thank you to keep to yourself, Mr. Thomas Sawyer. I'll never speak to *you* again." She then tossed her head and walked on.

Tom was so stunned that he didn't even think to say, "Who cares, Miss Smarty?" until long after she had left him. Instead, he moped into the schoolyard feeling angrier and angrier and even wishing she were a boy, and how he would trounce her in a fight if she were.

But Becky would soon enough find herself in trouble. Every day, their schoolmaster, Mr. Dobbins, would take a mysterious book out of his desk. The book was his prize possession, and he kept it under lock and key and read it when the class was busy. Every child in the school had a different theory about the book, and all of them were dying to get a glimpse at it.

Now, as Becky was passing Dobbins' desk, she noticed that the key was in the lock! The next instant she had the book in her hands. The title page—Professor Somebody's *History of Old England*—meant nothing to her, so she began to turn the pages. The first thing she saw was a handsomely engraved color image of a knight in armor sitting on his horse. Just then, a shadow fell on the page. Tom Sawyer was behind her. Becky quickly grabbed the book to close it. In doing so, she tore the picture half down the middle. She put the book back into Dobbins' desk, turned the key, and burst out crying with anger.

"Tom Sawyer, you are just as mean as can be, to sneak up on a person and look at what they're looking at."

"How could I know you was looking at anything?"

"You ought to be ashamed of yourself, Tom Sawyer; now you're going to tell on me. Oh, what shall I do, what shall I do! I've never been punished in school."

And with that she ran out of the room.

Tom, however, stood still. Feeling rather flustered, he mumbled to himself: "What a curious kind of a fool girl she is. Well, of course I ain't going to tell old Dobbins on this little fool, but what of it? He'll ask who tore his book. Nobody'll answer. Then he'll do just as he always does, asking one and then the other and when he comes to the right girl he'll know it, without any telling. Girls' faces always tell on them. They ain't got any backbone. So let her sweat it out."

Tom then joined a mob of his classmates who were chattering and playing games outside. A few moments later, schoolmaster Dobbins arrived, and all his pupils quieted down and followed him inside. Class started but Tom was too distracted by his latest fight to pay attention. He kept looking at the girls' side of the room, and Becky's worried face troubled him. He did not want to feel sorry for her, but he couldn't help it.

A whole hour somehow drifted past. By and by, Mr. Dobbins yawned, unlocked his desk, and reached for his book. As soon as he took it out of the desk, Tom shot a look at Becky. Her face reminded him of how a rabbit looks when a hound dog starts chasing it. Instantly, he forgot his fight with her. Something must be done and done quick! But what? He racked his brain but came up with nothing. There was a brief silence, long enough to count to ten. Then the schoolmaster spoke:

"Who tore this book?"

There wasn't a single sound as Dobbins searched face after face for signs of guilt.

"Benjamin Rogers, did you tear this book?"

"No sir."

"Joseph Harper, did you?"

Another denial.

The schoolmaster scanned the ranks of the boys—thought awhile—and then turned to the girls.

"Amy Lawrence?"

A shake of the head, and then, "No."

"Gracie Miller?"

The same reply.

"Susan Harper, did you do this?"

Another "No."

The next girl was Becky. Tom was trembling from head to toe.

"Rebecca Thatcher?"

Becky's face was white with terror. The poor

girl tried to turn away from Dobbins' stare, but he said, "Miss Thatcher, look me in the face and tell me, did you tear this book?"

A thought like lightning shot through Tom's brain. He sprang to his feet and shouted—"*I done it!*"

No one in the school could believe this amazing act of folly. But the look of gratitude and love that now shone from Becky's eyes was enough reward for a hundred lickings. Strengthened by that look, Tom took his punishment, and also the added cruelty of two hours' detention after school, without a single word of protest. He did so knowing who would be waiting for him outside, once detention was over.

That night, Tom fell asleep with Becky's words still echoing dreamily in his ear:

"Tom, how *could* you be so noble?"

CHAPTER 8

The Trial of Muff Potter

Summer vacation was fast approaching. The next thing Tom knew, school was over, and his days were free again. The Fourth of July came and went with little fanfare. Tom began to find his precious vacation time hanging heavy on his hands. First, Becky Thatcher had left town with her parents for a summer vacation. Then Tom came down with the measles.

During two long weeks, Tom lay in bed a prisoner, dead to the world and its happenings. When he finally got onto his feet, the town of St.

Petersburg had started to come back to life. Muff Potter's murder trial was ready to begin, and it soon became the talk of the town.

Every mention of the death of Dr. Robinson sent a shudder straight to Tom's heart. He didn't see how he could be suspected of knowing anything about it, but he still didn't feel comfortable in the midst of all the gossip. Just hearing the name "Muff Potter" kept him in a cold shiver. Tom ached to be rid of his terrible secret and to tell the truth. One day, he took Huck aside for a private talk.

"Huck," he started gravely. "Have you ever told anybody about—that?"

"About what?"

"You know what."

"Oh—course I haven't."

"Not a word?"

"Not a single word, so help me. What makes you ask?"

"Well, I was afraid."

"Why, Tom Sawyer, we wouldn't be alive two days if that got found out. *You* know that."

Tom paused for a moment.

"I reckon Muff Potter's a goner. Don't you feel sorry for him sometimes?"

"Most always," Huck responded. "Muff Potter ain't ever done anything to hurt anybody. Just fishes a little to get money and loafs around. But we all do that. He's kind of good, and he gave me half a fish once, when there wasn't enough for two; and lots of times he stood by me when I was out of luck."

"Well, he's helped fix kites for me when they got torn," Tom added. "And he tied hooks onto my fishing line when I couldn't do it. I wish we could get him out of jail."

"My! we couldn't get him out, Tom. And besides, it wouldn't do any good. They'd catch him again."

"They probably would," Tom agreed. "I just hate to hear how they abuse him so, 'specially as he hasn't done anything."

"I do, too, Tom. I hear 'em say that Muff's the bloodiest-looking villain in the country, and they wonder why he wasn't ever hung before."

The boys kept on talking, but it brought them little comfort. Tom went home miserable that night, and his dreams were full of horrors. The two next days, he hung about the court-room, drawn by an almost irresistible urge to go inside. Huck felt the same way. But both boys were too afraid, and they even avoided looking at each other.

Outside the courthouse, all the talk that Tom heard was about how things were looking bleak for Muff. At the end of the trial's second day, Injun Joe's evidence stood firm. There was not the slightest doubt as to what the verdict would be.

Tom was out late that night and came to bed through the window. He was in a terrible state of excitement and couldn't get to sleep for hours.

The next morning, the entire village flocked to the courthouse, for this was to be the great day. After a long wait, the jury filed in and took their places. Shortly afterward, Potter, looking pale and sleepless, was brought in with chains upon him and seated where everyone could stare at him. No less visible was Injun Joe, calm as ever. Once the judge arrived, the usual whisperings among the lawyers and shuffling of papers followed. All these details and delays in beginning the trial worked up an even greater feeling of suspense inside the courtroom.

Finally, a witness was called who testified that he had found Muff Potter washing in the creek, at an early hour of the morning that the murder was discovered, and that Muff had sneaked away immediately. After the prosecutor finished with his questions, it was time for Potter's lawyer to examine the witness.

"No questions," he said coolly.

The next witness said that he had found Muff Potter's knife near the dead body.

But again, Potter's lawyer didn't ask the man a single question.

A third and a fourth witness testified without Potter's lawyer doing anything. Meanwhile, members of the court audience became angry, and many started to wonder about what was really going on. Did Muff's attorney mean to throw away his client's life without an effort?

A final witness was called, and he testified to Potter's guilty behavior at the scene of the murder. Again, there were no questions from Potter's lawyer.

The crowd was quite restless now, and the

judge had to tell everyone to settle down. Finally, the prosecutor ended his case against Muff, saying:

"By the oaths of the citizens whose word can't be doubted, we have proved that this awful crime was carried out by the unhappy prisoner before you."

A groan escaped from poor Potter, and he put his face in his hands, rocking his body softly to and fro, while a painful silence filled the courtroom. Muff's lawyer then rose from his seat and said:

"Your Honor, at the beginning of this trial we stated our intent to prove that our client did this fearful deed while under the influence of a blind and irresponsible confusion caused by his dizzy spells. We have now changed our mind and shall offer proof of our client's innocence. We call Thomas Sawyer to the stand!"

Every face in the courthouse, including

Muff's, took on a look of puzzled astonishment as Tom rose and took his place in the witness stand. After the scared-looking boy raised his right hand and swore to tell the truth, Potter's lawyer looked him right in the eye.

"Thomas Sawyer, where were you on the seventeenth of June, about the hour of midnight?"

Tom glanced at Injun Joe's iron face, and his voice failed him. The audience listened breathless, but the words refused to come. After a few moments, he finally spoke out in a weak voice.

"In the graveyard!"

An evil-looking sneer passed across Injun Joe's face.

"Were you anywhere near Hoss Williams' grave?"

"Yes, sir."

"Speak up—just a little louder. How near were you?"

"As near as I am to you."

"Were you hidden or not?"

"I was hid."

"Where?"

"Behind the elms that's on the edge of the grave."

At that moment, Injun Joe's entire body seemed to tighten up, and the sneer on his face vanished.

"Anyone with you?"

"Yes sir. I went there with—"

"Wait a moment. Never mind your companion's name. We will introduce him at the proper time. Did you carry anything with you?"

Tom hesitated and looked confused.

"Speak out, my boy. The truth is always respectable. What did you take out there?"

"Only a—a potion, a potion to cure warts."

There was a ripple of laughter in the crowd.

"Now, my boy, tell us everything that occurred—tell it in your own way—don't skip over anything and don't be afraid."

Tom began—slowly at first, but as he warmed to his story, his words flowed more and more easily. In a little while, every sound ceased except for his own voice; every eye was fixed only on him. The tension inside the court reached its high point when the boy said:

"—and just after the doctor picked the board and hit Muff Potter and Muff fell, Injun Joe jumped with the knife and—"

Crash! Quick as lightning, Injun Joe tore his way through the crowd, sprang for the window, and was gone!

CHAPTER 9

Seeking Buried Treasure

～∽

Tom was a hero—the envy of young and old alike. His name was even in the St. Petersburg town paper. But as happy as Tom's days now were, his nights were filled with fear. Injun Joe lurked in all of his dreams, always with doom in his eye.

Poor Huck felt as afraid as Tom and was desperately worried that Injun Joe might discover his own role and come after him, too. Tom's sense of right and wrong had made him secretly visit Muff Potter's lawyer and tell him what really happened. But by doing so, Tom also had betrayed a blood oath, the most secret of all oaths. After that, Huck found it hard to have much faith in anything anymore.

After the trial's dramatic end, rewards had been offered for Injun Joe's capture. The country had been searched high and low, but he was nowhere to be found. As the days drifted on without any sign of Injun Joe, Tom felt less and less scared.

Soon, he had an idea to dig for hidden treasure. Tom now sought out Huck, who, he knew, was always willing to take part in any plan that seemed exciting. Huck jumped at Tom's offer, but after thinking a moment he asked, "Where'll we dig, Tom?"

"Oh, most anywhere," Tom replied.

"Why, is treasure hid all around?"

"No, indeed it ain't. It's hid in mighty particular places, Huck—sometimes on islands, sometimes in rotten chests under the limb of an old dead tree, just where the shadow falls at midnight. Mostly it's hid under the floor in haunted houses."

"Who hides it?"

"Why, robbers of course—who'd you reckon? Sunday school teachers?"

"If I was a robber, I wouldn't hide it; I'd spend it and have a good time."

"So would I. But robbers don't do it that way. They always hide it and leave it there."

"Don't they come after it anymore?"

"They think they will but they generally forget where they put the treasure map with the marks to show them just where to dig. Or sometimes they die. So the treasure just sits there a long time and gets rusty. By and by, somebody finds an old yellow paper map that tells how to find the marks."

"Have you got one of them maps, Tom?"

"No."

"Well then, how are you going to find them marks?"

"Forget the marks. They always bury it under a haunted house, or on an island, or under a dead tree that's got one limb sticking out. There's the old haunted house up around Cardiff Hill, and there's lots of dead-limb trees, too."

"There's an awful lot of dead trees around these parts, Tom. How you going to know which one to go for?"

"Go for all of 'em!"

"Why, Tom, it'll take all summer."

"Well, what of it? Suppose you find a brass pot with a hundred dollars in it, all rusty and gray, or a rotten chest full of diamonds. How's that for a summer's work?"

Huck's eyes glowed. That was all the convincing he needed.

"Suppose we tackle that old dead-limb tree

way up on Cardiff Hill on the other side of the creek?" Huck suggested.

"I'm agreed."

So the boys got a pick and a shovel and set out on their trek. When they finally arrived at the old dead tree, hot and panting, they sat down in the shade of a neighboring elm to rest and chew gum.

"I like this," said Tom.

"So do I," Huck agreed.

"Say, Huck, if we find a treasure here, what are you going to do with your share?"

"Well, I'll have a pie and a soda every day, and I'll go to every circus that comes along."

"Ain't you going to save any of it?"

"Save it. What for?"

"Well, what if you want to get married."

"Married!"

"That's right."

"Tom, you—why, you ain't in your right mind."

"Wait—you'll see."

"Tom, that's about the most foolish thing you could do. Look at my pa and my ma. Why, they used to fight all the time. I remember, mighty well."

"The girl I'm going to marry won't fight."

"Tom, you better think this out awhile. They *all* like to fight. What's the name of this gal?"

"I'll tell you sometime—not now."

"All right—that'll do. Only if you get married, I'll be more lonesome than ever."

"No, you won't. You'll come and live with me. Now, let's start digging."

They worked and sweated for half an hour. No result. They toiled another half hour. Still nothing.

"Do they always bury treasure as deep as this?" Huck asked.

"Not generally. I reckon we haven't got the right place."

So they chose a new spot and began digging again. Finally, Huck leaned on his shovel, swabbed the beaded drops of sweat from his brow with his sleeve, and said:

"Heck, Tom, we must be in the wrong place again. What do you think?"

"It *is* mighty curious. I reckon maybe there's a witch making trouble for us 'cause witches like to keep the gold hid for themselves."

"Shucks, witches ain't got no power in the daytime."

"Well, that's so," Tom admitted. "I didn't think of that. Oh, *I* know what's wrong! What fools we are! You've got to find out where the shadow of the dead-limb tree falls exactly at the stroke of midnight by the light of the moon, and then that's where you dig!"

"Confound it," Huck moaned. "We've did all this work for nothing."

"We've got to do it tonight, that's all," Tom responded.

"Can you get out?" Huck asked.

"I bet I will."

"Well, I'll come around and meow like a cat tonight."

"All right," Tom said. "Let's hide the tools in the bushes."

Late that night, the two boys sneaked back to the old dead tree and sat in shadow waiting for midnight. It was a lonely place where spirits whispered in the rustling leaves, and ghosts lurked in the murky nooks. The deep baying of a hound floated out of the distance, and an owl answered with a low hoot. Finally, Tom and Huck judged that the hour of twelve had come at last. They marked the spot where the shadow fell and began to dig. The holes grew deeper and deeper, but every time they heard their picks strike something, it turned out to be just a stone.

"It ain't any use," Tom said. "Huck, we're wrong again."

"But we *can't* be wrong. We marked the shadow exact."

"Well, there's one other thing," Tom said slowly.

"What's that?"

"We only guessed at the time 'cause we don't have a watch. It must have been too late or too early."

Huck dropped his shovel.

"That's it," he said. "We've got to give up on this one; we'll never be able to tell the right time. Besides, this time of night's too awful, full of witches and ghosts a-fluttering around us. I feel as if something's behind me most all the time."

"I've been feeling pretty much the same way," Tom confessed.

"Say, Tom, let's give this place up and try somewhere else."

"I reckon we'd better."

"What'll it be?"

Tom considered awhile, and then said:

"The haunted house. That's it!"

"Dang it, Tom, I don't like haunted houses. There's liable to be twice as many ghosts in there."

"Yes, but Huck, ghosts travel only at night. They won't stop us digging there in the daytime."

"Well, that's so," Huck had to agree. "But you know mighty well, people don't go about that haunted house day or night."

"That's mostly because they don't like to go where a man's been killed. Anyway, nothing's ever been seen around that house except at night—just some blue lights slipping by the windows—no regular ghosts."

"Well, Tom, wherever you see them blue

lights flickering, you can bet there's a ghost mighty close by. It stands to reason."

"That's so," Tom agreed. "But ghosts don't come around in the daytime, so what's the use of being all afraid?"

"Well, all right. We'll tackle the haunted house if you say so. But I reckon it's taking chances."

By this time they had already started walking down the hill. There in the middle of the moonlit valley below stood the haunted house with its fences long gone and thick weeds smothering the doorsteps. The chimney had fallen down, the window sashes were torn to pieces, and even a corner of the roof had caved in. The boys gazed at the house for a while, half expecting to see a blue light flit past the windows at any moment. Then, talking in a low tone, they made a sharp right turn to get as far away as they could from it, and took their way homeward through the woods that covered the back slope of Cardiff Hill.

CHAPTER 10

Danger Inside the Haunted House

⌒

By noon the next day, the boys were back at the haunted house. There was something so strange about the dead silence that ruled there under the baking sun, and something so sad about the loneliness of the place, that they were afraid to go in. Finally, they crept to a window and took a trembling peep. Inside, they saw a weed-grown and floorless room, an ancient fireplace, and a broken-down staircase. Ragged cobwebs hung everywhere.

Tom and Huck entered, softly, talking in

whispers, ears alert for the slightest sound, and muscles ready for an instant retreat. They gave the grounds a thorough search, growing less and less afraid all the while. Finally, they put their digging tools aside and decided to look upstairs.

It proved just as dark and dirty as the floor below. In one corner, they found a closet, but it turned out to be empty. Disappointed, they were about to go down and begin work when—

"Shush!" said Tom.

"What is it?" Huck whispered, turning white with fright.

"There! . . . Hear it?"

"Yes! . . . Oh, my! Let's run!"

"Keep still!" Tom said. "They're coming right toward the front door."

The boys stretched themselves upon the floor, peering through some broken boards

down on the room below. They lay there, as still as could be, waiting in fear.

The front door swung open, and two men entered. Tom turned to Huck and softly muttered: "There's the old Spanish man that's been about town once or twice lately. They say he can't talk or hear. I've never seen the other man before."

"The other man" was a ragged, dirty-looking fellow with a dark scowl on his face. As for the mysterious Spaniard, he had wrapped himself in a long blanket called a serape. He had bushy white whiskers; long white hair flowed from under his sombrero, and he wore green goggles. Both men sat down on the ground, facing the door, with their backs to the wall, while Tom and Huck tried to hear every word they were saying.

"No," said the scowling man to his companion. "I've thought it over, and I don't like it. It's dangerous."

"Dangerous!" grunted the Spaniard, shocking the boys by speaking. "Humbug!"

As soon as Tom and Huck heard the voice, they both started to shake. It was Injun Joe in disguise! There was a long pause. Then Joe said: "What's more dangerous than coming here in the daytime!"

"*I* know that. I want to quit this dump, and the sooner the better."

The two men unpacked some food and started to prepare lunch. After a thoughtful silence, Injun Joe said:

"Look here, lad—you go back up the river where you belong. Wait there till you hear from me. I'll take the chances on dropping into this town just once more, for a look. We'll do that 'dangerous' job after I've spied around a little. Then we're off for Texas!"

Once the other man agreed, they ate their

lunch in silence. Afterward, they both began yawning. Injun Joe said:

"I need some sleep! It's your turn to watch."

Joe curled down in the weeds and soon began to snore. A little while later, the lookout began to nod as well. His head drooped lower and lower. Soon, both men were fast asleep.

The boys drew a long, grateful breath. Tom whispered:

"Now's our chance—come on."

"I can't," Huck said, his voice shaking. "I'd die if they was to wake."

Tom rose slowly, but the first step he took made such a loud creak from the crazy floor that he sank down almost dead with fright. Both boys lay there frozen, counting the seconds. Finally, they noticed the sun starting to set.

Suddenly, Injun Joe stopped snoring, sat up, and looked around.

"Hey, *you're* a watchman, ain't you?" Joe said

with a smile, poking the other man with his foot.

"My!" the man gulped. "Have I been asleep?"

Joe laughed.

"Nearly time for us to be moving, partner. What'll we do with the stolen money we've got left?"

"I don't know—leave it here as we've always done, I reckon. Six hundred silver dollars is something to carry!"

"Okay," Injun Joe agreed, "but this time we bury it, bury it deep."

"Good idea," said Joe's comrade, who walked across the room, knelt down, picked up one of the heavy stones by the broken-down fireplace, and pulled out a bag of coins. He took twenty or thirty dollars from it for himself and as much for Injun Joe. He then passed the bag to Joe, who was now on his knees in the corner digging with his bowie knife.

At the sight of the gleaming coins, Tom and

Huck suddenly forgot all their fears. What luck! Six hundred dollars was enough money to make half a dozen boys rich! Here was treasure hunting at its best—you knew just where to dig!

Joe's knife struck something.

"What's that?" asked the other man.

"Half-rotten plank—no, it's a box, I believe. Wait." Joe reached his hand in and drew it out— "Man, it's money!"

The two men examined the handful of gold coins. The boys above were equally delighted.

"We'll make quick work of this," Joe said. "There's an old rusty pick on the other side of the fireplace. I saw it a minute ago."

He ran and brought back the boys' pick and shovel, and in a few moments the two men unearthed a box. It was small and made of iron but covered with rust from sitting there all these years. The men looked at the treasure in silence, hardly believing what they saw.

"Partner, there's thousands of dollars here," said Injun Joe.

"I always heard it said that old Tom Murrel's gang of bank robbers used to be around here one summer," his friend added.

"I know it," said Injun Joe. "And this looks like it, I should say."

"*Now* you won't need to do that last job."

Injun Joe frowned.

"You don't know me." Joe's eyes became hard and cold. "The job ain't about robbery. It's personal. It's about *revenge*! I'll need your help in it. When it's finished—then Texas. Now go home and wait there until you hear from me."

"Well—if you say so." Then the man asked, "What should we do with the box? Shall we bury it again?"

When Injun Joe said "Yes," Tom and Huck could hardly conceal their delight. But then, after a few seconds, Joe cried out "No!" and the boys couldn't have felt glummer. But their gloom quickly turned to terror when Injun Joe then said, "That pick had fresh earth on it! What business have a pick and a shovel here? With fresh earth on them, no less. Who brought them here—and where are they gone? Have you heard anybody? Seen anybody? What! bury it again and let them come and see the ground disturbed? Not exactly—not exactly. We'll take this back to my den."

"Why, of course! I might have thought of that. You mean Number One?"

"No—Number Two—under the cross. The other place is bad—too obvious."

Desperate, the boys prayed that Injun Joe and his partner would give them some clue about where the hiding place they were talking about was, and what Injun Joe meant when he said he would conceal the treasure "under the cross." Under what cross?

Instead, however, the other man said to Joe, "All right. It's nearly dark enough to start out. We had better get moving."

Joe got up and went to each window, cautiously peeping out to see if anyone was outside. Then he said:

"Who could have brought those tools here? Do you reckon they could be upstairs?"

Injun Joe put his hand on his knife, halted a moment, and then headed toward the stairway. Tom and Huck were so scared now that they could hardly breathe. They thought of hiding in the closet, but their strength was gone. All they could do was listen to the sound of steps come creaking up the stairs when there was a sudden crash of rotten timbers as Injun Joe tumbled to the ground amid the debris of the ruined stairway.

"Now, what's the use of all that?" Joe's accomplice asked. "If there's anybody up there, let 'em *stay* up there—who cares? It'll be dark in fifteen minutes—and then let them follow us if they want to. In my view, whoever brought the pick and shovel in here caught a sight of us and took us for ghosts or devils or something and ran off. I bet they're still running."

Joe grumbled a while before agreeing with his partner. The men got their things ready, including the precious iron box, and quietly slipped out of the house and into the darkening twilight.

CHAPTER 11

On the Trail of Injun Joe

⤳

The adventure of the day tormented Tom's dreams that night. Four times he laid his hands on that rich treasure, and four times it slipped away. When he woke up, Tom decided maybe it *was* just a dream. As soon as he finished breakfast, Tom went to find Huck Finn. If it was a dream, Huck would know for sure.

Tom found his friend sitting on the deck of a boat, dangling his feet in the water and looking quite sad.

"Hello, Huck!" Tom said cheerfully.

"Hello, yourself."

Silence for a minute.

"Tom, if we'd a' left the blame tools at the dead tree, we'd a' got the money. Oh, ain't it awful!"

"'Tain't a dream then, 'tain't a dream! Somehow I wished it was."

"What ain't a dream?"

"Oh, that whole thing yesterday. I half figured it was."

"A dream! If them stairs hadn't broke down you'd a' seen how much of a dream it was. I've been dreaming of that devil Injun Joe all night. Curse him!"

"No, Huck, not curse him. *Find* him. We've got to find him and track him out to his 'Number Two.'"

"I been thinking about that. But I can't make anything out of it. What do you reckon it is?"

"I don't know. It's too deep. Say, Huck, maybe it's the number of a house."

"No, Tom. That ain't it. There ain't no numbers in this one-horse town."

"Wait now, lemme think a minute. It's the number of a room—in an inn, you know!"

"Oh, that's the trick! They ain't only two inns. We can find out quick."

A half hour later, the boys had been to both places. In the best inn, a young lawyer had long occupied room number 2. In the shabbier lodge, room number 2 was a mystery. The innkeeper's young son said it was locked all the time, and nobody came in or out of it except at night.

The boys decided that this must be the place they were looking for. Tom quickly came up with a plan. They would get hold of all the door keys they could find and wait for a dark night to try them. As simple as that, the treasure would be theirs.

That night Tom and Huck hung about in the neighborhood of the inn until after nine, one watching the alley and the other the inn door. No one who looked like the "Spaniard" entered or left.

Tuesday and Wednesday brought the same poor luck. But Thursday night promised better. Tom slipped out of his house with Aunt Polly's old tin lantern and a large towel to blindfold it with. An hour before midnight, the inn closed up and its lights were put out. Nobody had entered or left the alley. The black of night was all around, the perfect stillness interrupted only by the mutter of distant thunder.

Tom lit his lantern and wrapped it closely in the towel. The boys crept silently in the gloom toward the inn. Huck stood guard as Tom felt his way into the pitch-black alley. Some minutes passed as Huck kept watch, but there was no sight of Tom. Huck found himself drifting closer and closer to the alley, fearing all sorts of dreadful things. Suddenly there was a flash of light and Tom came tearing by him:

"Run!" he said. "Run for your life!"

The two boys didn't stop running until they reached a deserted barn. As soon as Tom got his breath, he said:

"Huck, it was awful! I tried two of the keys just as quiet as I could! But they made such a racket that I couldn't hardly breathe. Without even noticing what I was doing, I took hold of the knob, and open comes the door! It wasn't even locked. I hopped in, shook off the towel, and *great Caesar's ghost!*"

"What—what'd you see, Tom?"

"Huck, I almost stepped onto Injun Joe's hand!"

"No!"

"Yes! He was laying there, sound asleep on the floor with his arms spread out."

"Did he wake up?"

"No, never budged."

"Say, Tom, did you see that box?"

"Huck, I didn't wait to look around. I didn't see the box. I didn't see the cross. I didn't see anything but a tin cup on the floor by Injun Joe."

After thinking for a moment, Tom continued:

"Looky-here, Huck. Let's not try anything else until we know Injun Joe's not in there. It's too scary. If we watch every night, we'll be sure to see him go out sometime or another and then we'll snatch that box quicker than lightning."

Huck said he'd watch the tavern every night if, when the time came, Tom would do the snatching. And so off they went, each one dreaming of the riches that would soon be theirs.

CHAPTER 12

Huck's a Hero

The first thing Tom heard on Friday morning was a glad piece of news—Becky Thatcher and her family had finally come back to town from their summer holiday. Tom saw Becky right away, and they had a great time playing games with their schoolmates. Becky then convinced her mother to choose the next day for a long-promised and long-delayed school picnic.

Next morning a rowdy group of youngsters gathered outside Judge Thatcher's house. An old steamboat had been chartered for the all-day trip and, presently, the happy throng of children, laden with baskets of food, made their way to the boat.

"You'll not get back till late," Mrs. Thatcher said to Becky, as the children prepared to leave. "You'd better stay the night with some of the girls who live near the ferry landing."

"I'll stay with Susie Harper, Mamma."

"Very well. And mind you don't be any trouble."

As Tom raced along with Becky and the other children toward the ferry, he thought suddenly of Huck, that he might come that very night and give Tom a signal that Injun Joe's room was empty. Still, the signal hadn't come the night before, so why should it be any more likely to come tonight?

Three miles below town, the ferryboat stopped at the mouth of a woody hollow. The crowd of happy children swarmed ashore, and soon the forest distances and rocky heights echoed far and near with shouting and laughter. All the different ways of getting hot and tired were fully explored before the picnickers straggled back to the camp with mighty appetites. After much feasting, it now was time to explore McDougal's cave.

Candles were brought, and the whole group scampered up the hill. The cave's entrance was up the hillside, and its massive oak door stood wide open. It was breathtaking to stand there in the deep gloom at the cave's mouth and look out upon the green valley shining in the sun.

By and by the procession of children began filing down the

steep descent of the cave's main passage, their flickering rank of lights dimly revealing the lofty walls of rock surrounding them. It was no more than ten feet wide, and narrower crevices branched off it every few feet. It was said that one might wander days and nights through this vast tangle of rifts and chasms and never find the end of it.

After awhile, some of the children began to sneak away from the larger group and play hide and seek in the explored areas of the cave before straggling back toward the mouth of the cavern, panting for breath, laughing, smeared head to toe with candle drippings, daubed with clay, and delighted with their adventure. They arrived just in time; the bell had been clanging, and the ferryboat was set to return to town.

An hour later, Huck was just starting on his watch when he saw the ferryboat's lights go glinting past the wharf. He wondered what boat it was and why it didn't stop at the wharf. But he didn't wonder long. The night was growing dark, and he had business to attend to.

Ten o'clock came, and the noise of vehicles ceased. Scattered lights also began to go out, and the streets grew empty. By eleven o'clock, darkness was everywhere. Huck waited for what seemed like a weary long time, but nothing happened. Was there really any use in staying longer? he wondered. Why not give it up and turn in?

Then a noise fell upon his ear. The alley door closed softly. Huck sprang to the corner of a closed barbershop. The next moment two men brushed by him, and one seemed to have something under his arm. The box! They were going to remove the treasure! Huck's mind was racing. The men would get away with the box and never be found again. No, he would follow them himself.

Huck stepped out and glided behind the men, cat-like, with bare feet, allowing them to keep just far enough ahead so as not to be invisible.

They moved along River Street three blocks and then turned left. They went up the path to Cardiff Hill, passed by the old Welshman's cabin halfway up the hill, and still kept climbing. "Good," Huck thought, "they will bury the box in the old quarry. But the men didn't stop at the quarry." They passed on, up the summit, and plunged into the narrow path between the tall sumac bushes. Huck shortened his distance; it was too dark now for the men to see him. He trotted along a while and then stopped. He listened but heard no sound, none but the beating of his own heart. Huck was again about to give up, when a man cleared his throat not four feet away!

Huck stood there shaking badly. He knew just where he was: within five feet of the pathway leading to the Widow Douglas's house. Let them bury it there; it would be hard to find.

Now there was a voice—a very low voice—Injun Joe's:

"Look, there's lights. Maybe she's got company."

"I can't see any."

Huck recognized the sound of Joe's partner. A dead chill shot through him—this was the "revenge" job! He remembered that the Widow Douglas's husband had been the justice of the peace and had arrested Injun Joe countless times. Now Joe and his partner were planning to get revenge on his widow by robbing her, or worse!

Huck held his breath and slowly took one step back, then another. After he'd gone far enough away, he started flying down the hill. Down, down he sped till he reached the old Welshman's cabin. Huck banged loudly at the door, and soon the heads of the old men and his two strong sons appeared in the windows.

"What's the row there? Who's banging? What do you want?"

"Huckleberry Finn—quick, let me in!"

"Huckleberry Finn, indeed! It ain't a name to open many doors. But let him in, lads, and let's see what's the trouble."

"Please don't ever tell *I* told you," were Huck's first words when he got in. "But the Widow Douglas has been good to me sometimes. I want to tell—I *will* tell if you'll promise you won't even say it was me."

"By George, he *has* got something to tell, or he wouldn't act so!" exclaimed the old man. "Out with it and nobody here will ever tell, lad."

Three minutes later the old man and his sons, well armed, were up the hill right by the sumac path. Huck left them there and hid behind a great boulder. After a few moments of tense silence, all of a sudden the small boy heard an explosion of guns and a cry.

Huck didn't wait to find out what had happened. He sprang away and sped down the hill as fast as his legs could carry him.

CHAPTER 13

Trapped in the Cave

~

That Sunday morning, as soon as dawn broke, Huck again came racing up the hill and knocked gently at the old Welshman's door.

"Who's there?" a gruff voice shouted.

"Please let me in. It's only Huck Finn."

"That's a name that can open this door night or day, lad! Welcome."

The door was quickly unlocked. Huck was given a comfortable seat as the old man began preparing a hero's breakfast for him.

"The boys and I were hoping you'd stop back here last night."

"I was awful scared," said Huck. "I took off when the pistols went off, and I was a-feared to come back before it was light."

"Poor chap, you do look as if you've had a hard night. There's a bed here for you when you've had your breakfast. We came near to catching those devils last night. We would have had 'em if I hadn't sneezed. It was the worst kind of luck! Right off, those scoundrels started running. We fired away at them, but they were off in a jiffy. The sheriff got a posse together, and they're searching the woods. You couldn't see what they were like, in the dark, I suppose?"

"Oh, yes, I saw them downtown and followed them. One's the Spaniard that's been around here once or twice. The other's—"

"That's enough, lad. We know the men!

Off with you boys, and tell the sheriff!"

Just as the Welshman's sons were about to leave the room, Huck sprang up.

"Oh, please don't tell *anybody* it was me that told on 'em. Oh, please!"

"Huck, you ought to have the credit."

"Oh, no, no! Please don't tell!"

"They won't—and I won't. But why don't you want it known?"

Huck would not explain—other than that he was afraid. The old man promised secrecy once more.

"How did you come to follow these fellows? Were they looking suspicious?"

Huck was silent for a while, thinking of what to say.

"Well, you see, I couldn't sleep last night, and I saw these two men down by the inn and one of them was carrying something that looked stolen." He went on, quickly making up a story about how he decided to follow the men, one of whom he recognized as the Spaniard, up the hill and to the Widow Douglas' house.

"And then the Spaniard said—"

"What? The Spaniard can talk?"

Huck realized his mistake instantly. He made several feeble efforts to try to cover his tracks but the old man cut him off.

"My boy, don't be afraid of me. I wouldn't hurt a hair on your head for all the world. You know something about that Spaniard that you want to keep secret. Now trust me, lad, tell me the rest. I won't betray you."

Huck looked into the old man's honest eyes a moment, then he whispered in his ear:

"'Tain't a Spaniard—it's Injun Joe!"

The Welshman almost jumped out of his chair. After a moment, he said:

"It's all clear now. Injun Joe always held it against the widow's husband for putting him in jail all the time."

Huck sat down to breakfast feeling faint. He was mad at himself for being so nervous and letting the information about Injun Joe slip. At the same time, he felt relieved. The Welshman told the rest of the story: how the scoundrels had dropped a bunch of burglar tools when they ran. There was no mention of treasure, which, Huck thought, must mean that it was still back in the room in the inn. Injun Joe and his friend would be captured and jailed that day, Huck figured. Then he and Tom could seize the gold that very night without any trouble at all.

Everyone in St. Petersburg went early to church that morning. The town was buzzing with the news from the night before. The word was that not a sign of the two villains had been found. When the sermon was finished, Judge

Thatcher's wife dropped alongside of Mrs. Harper as she moved down the aisle with the crowd and said:

"Is my Becky going to sleep all day? I just expected she would be tired to death."

"Your Becky?"

"Yes. Didn't she stay with you last night?"

"Why, no."

Mrs. Thatcher turned pale and sank into a pew. Just then Tom's Aunt Polly passed by and said:

"Good morning, Mrs. Thatcher. Good morning, Mrs. Harper. I reckon my Tom must have stayed at your house last night—or with you, Mrs. Harper. And now he's afraid to come to church. I've got to settle with him."

Mrs. Thatcher shook her head feebly, and her face turned pale.

"He didn't stay with us," said Mrs. Harper, beginning to look uneasy.

The news quickly made the rounds, but no one could remember the last time they'd seen either Tom or Becky. None of the children had even noticed if they were aboard the ferryboat for the homeward trip. One young man finally blurted out his fear that they were still in the cave! Mrs. Thatcher fainted and Aunt Polly fell to crying and wringing her hands.

Within minutes, horses were saddled; the ferryboat was ordered out; and in less than one-half hour, two hundred men were pouring down the river toward the cave.

All that night the town waited for news; but when the morning dawned at last, the children had still not been found. Finally, early Monday afternoon, parties of weary men began to straggle back into the village. In one remote place, far from the section usually visited by tourists, the names BECKY & TOM had been found traced upon a rocky wall with candle smoke. That was the nearest the searchers had come to the two lost children.

Tom and Becky were there all right, hopelessly lost deep in the cave's innermost recesses. After hide and go seek, they had wandered carelessly through the cave looking at the names and dates that had been left on the rock walls. They both then descended into the secret depths of the abyss, with Tom making smoke marks all the way along so they wouldn't get lost. Finally, they came upon a huge cavern. Here, under the roof, vast knots of bats had packed themselves together, thousands in a bunch. The candlelight startled the creatures, and they came flocking down by the hundreds, squeaking and darting furiously at the bright lights. In a panic, Tom seized Becky's hands and they raced into the first corridor that Tom saw. The bats chased the children a good distance, but Tom and Becky kept running into every new passage they saw until they finally got rid of the frightening creatures. When they stopped to get their bearings, they found they were on the shore of a vast underground lake. Tom was then overtaken by a terrible fear.

"Can you find the way out?" Becky asked hopefully.

"I reckon I can find it," Tom said carefully, noticing that the bats had put out Becky's candle. "But the bats—if they put out both of our candles it will be an awful fix. Let's try some other way, so as not to go through there."

They started down another corridor, walking in silence for a long time and glancing at each new opening for signs of anything that looked familiar. Each time Tom explored one of the corridors, his face grew less and less hopeful.

"All is lost," Becky cried fearfully, clinging to Tom's arm after they'd been walking for some time. "Oh, Tom, never mind the bats," she pleaded. "Let's go back that way!"

Tom agreed, but now he couldn't find the way back. Each turn was the wrong turn. Becky got more and more worried until finally Tom broke down and said,

"Becky, I was such a fool! I didn't make any marks, and now I can't find the way back."

Becky sank to the ground and burst into a frenzy of crying that shook Tom's bones. They searched around a bit more and traced the sound of dripping water to a spring, where the two children finally collapsed, exhausted and terrified. The hours passed until finally they dozed off.

After waking, Becky suggested they move on again.

There was a long pause before Tom spoke.

"Becky, I have to tell you something. We must stay here where there's water to drink.

That little piece is our last candle!"

Becky again burst into tears. Tom did what he could to comfort her.

"They'll miss us and they'll hunt for us. It's certain they will," Tom said. The only question, he thought to himself, was how long would it take. While Becky wept, Tom saw the candle melt slowly away. Soon there was only the wick, and they watched as the feeble flames rose and fell, climbing the thin column of smoke, lingering at the top a moment, and then—the horror of utter darkness!

The hours wasted away. The children drifted off to sleep and woke up again. Soon hunger began to torment them. Tom was wondering how long they could last without food when—

"*Sh*! Did you hear that?"

Both held their breath and listened. There was a sound like the faintest, far-off shout. Instantly Tom answered it and, leading Becky by the hand, started groping down the corridor in its direction.

The sound was heard again, apparently a little nearer.

"They're coming!" Tom yelled. "Come along, Becky—we're all right now!"

Tom traced the sound slowly until they came to a couple of small side passages that led downward. He took a kite line from his pocket and tied it to a rock. Then he left Becky there and started down one of the passages.

At the end of twenty steps the corridor seemed to end, and Tom got down on his knees and felt as far around the corner of a large boulder as he could reach with his hands. Just at that moment, not twenty yards away, a human hand, holding a candle, appeared from behind a rock! Tom lifted up a glorious holler, and instantly that hand was followed by the body that it belonged to—Injun Joe!

Tom couldn't move. Luckily, Joe turned and took to his heels, running out of sight. Tom's

fright weakened every muscle in his body. He told himself that if he had enough strength to get back to the spring he would stay there, and nothing would tempt him to run the risk of meeting Injun Joe again.

But hunger and cold proved stronger than Tom's fears after another long night at the spring had passed. Now he felt willing to risk Injun Joe and all other terrors. But Becky was very weak and could not go with him. Tom kissed her on her forehead and made a show of being sure that he would find an escape from the cave. Then he took the kite line in his hand and once more went groping down one of the passages, feeling hungry and sick and with his mind filled with the thought of coming doom.

CHAPTER 14

Joyful News and a Great Surprise

❧

Tuesday night came and the whole village of St. Petersburg was in mourning. Most of the searchers had given up, and many people said the children could never be found. Then, in the middle of the night, a wild peal burst from the village bells, and the streets swarmed with frantic half-clad people who shouted:

"They're found! They're found!"

Aunt Polly began cheering and wildly clapping her hands while Mrs. Thatcher could barely speak; she was still crying but now she was raining tears of joy. Tom lay on a sofa with a crowd gathered around him and told the history of how he left Becky and went on alone to find an opening; how he followed two passages as far as his kite line would reach; how he followed a third to the fullest stretch of the kite line, and was about to turn back when he glimpsed a far-off speck that looked like daylight; how he then dropped the line and groped toward it, pushed his head and shoulders through a small hole, and saw the broad Mississippi River rolling by!

Three days and nights of toil and hunger were not to be shaken off easily; Tom and Becky were bedridden all of Wednesday and Thursday. Saturday was nearly spent when he finally got up and about.

Tom immediately went to see Huck, who had been laid up with a serious fever, but the Widow Douglas was caring for him and would allow no visitors.

A week later, Huck was still laid up. Tom stopped by to see Becky. Judge Thatcher and some friends set Tom to talking about his adventures in the cave.

"Well," the judge said when Tom was done, "nobody will get lost in that cave anymore."

"Why?" Tom asked.

"Because I had its big door covered with sheet iron two weeks ago, and had it triple locked—and I've got the keys."

Tom turned as white as a sheet.

"What's the matter, boy? Here, run, somebody! Fetch a glass of water!"

The water was brought and thrown into Tom's face.

"Ah, now you're all right. What was the matter with you?"

"Oh, Judge, Injun Joe's in the cave!"

A few hours later, the cave door was unlocked. Injun Joe lay stretched upon the ground dead, with his face close to the crack of the door. The poor unfortunate had starved to death.

After Huck was finally well, the two boys had a talk. There was still no news about the treasure. Injun Joe's room at the inn had been searched, but it had been empty.

"I reckon Injun Joe's left friends behind him," Huck said. "And they took the money. Anyways, it's a goner for us, Tom."

"Huck, that money wasn't ever in the inn!"

"What!"

"Huck, it's in the cave!"

Soon after, the boys borrowed a small boat and headed down the river. When they were several miles below the cave, Tom directed Huck to steer the boat ashore.

"Now, Huck, where we're a-standin' you could touch that hole I got out with a fishing pole. See if you can find it."

Huck searched all over the place but found

nothing. Tom proudly marched into a clump of sumac bushes and said:

"Here you are! Look at it, Huck; it's the snuggest hole in this country. All along, I've been wanting to be a robber but I knew I'd got to have a thing like this. We'll keep it quiet, only let Joe Harper know—because of course we need a gang. Tom Sawyer's Gang—it sounds splendid, don't it, Huck?"

"Well, it just does, Tom. And who'll we rob?"

"Oh, most anybody, I guess."

"Why, it sounds bully, Tom."

By this time the boys were ready to enter the hole, Tom in the lead. They worked their way to the far end of the tunnel. A few more steps brought them to the spring where Tom and Becky had stayed. Seeing it again, Tom felt a shudder of fear rush through him. He showed Huck the fragment of candlewick perched on a lump of clay against the wall and told how he and Becky had watched the flames flicker and die. They went on some yards farther to the place where Tom had first spotted Injun Joe.

"Now I'll show you something, Huck."

Tom held his candle high and said:

"Look as far around the corner as you can. Do you see that? There—on the big rock over yonder—done with the candle smoke."

"Tom, it's a *cross*!"

"*Now*, where's your Number Two? *Under the cross*, huh?"

The boys got their knives out and started digging. They hadn't gone four inches before they struck wood.

Huck began to dig and scratch; soon enough they'd unearthed the treasure box.

"Got it at last!" said Huck, opening the chest and running both his hands through the old coins. "We're rich!"

After packing the coins into bags, the two boys decided to hide the money in the loft of the

widow's woodshed and then bury it in the next
few days. They loaded up a wagon and were just
passing the Welshman's place when they decided
to rest. As they were about to move on, the old
man himself stepped out of his cabin.

"What luck! You boys are keeping everybody
waiting. Come along with me. Here—hurry
up—I'll haul the wagon for you. Hurry along,
hurry along!"

Tom and Huck wanted to know what the

rush was about, but there was no time to ask. Soon enough, they were at the Widow Douglas' home. A huge crowd was there, boasting everybody that was of any importance in the village. The widow welcomed the boys as heartily as anyone could welcome two such beings, both covered in clay, mud, and candle grease. Aunt Polly blushed crimson, shaking her head at Tom.

"Tom wasn't at home," the Welshman said. "So I gave up looking for him, but I stumbled on him and Huck right at my door, and I brought them along in a hurry."

"And you did just right," said the widow. "Come with me, boys."

Taking them upstairs, she continued, "Now, boys, wash and dress yourselves. Here are two new suits of clothes—shirts, socks, everything. They're Huck's but they'll fit both of you. Get into them. We'll wait—come down when you're slicked up enough."

CHAPTER 15

Respectable Huck Joins Tom's Gang

৩

Huck looked around nervously.

"That window ain't too high, Tom. If we can find a rope, I reckon we can scoot out of here."

"Shucks, what do you want to do that for?"

"I ain't used to that kind of crowd, Tom. I can't go down there."

"Oh, bother. It ain't anything. I'll take care of you."

Some minutes later, the widow's guests were at the supper table, and a dozen children were propped up at little side tables in the room. The dinner was in honor of the old Welshman and his sons to thank them for their heroic deeds. At the proper time, the old man got to his feet to make a speech and thank the widow. As the crowd listened eagerly, he paused and then said there was another person in the room who deserved the greatest honor.

"Huck Finn."

A murmur of surprise ran through the room. The widow herself wore a look of great astonishment as she now learned of Huck's role in preventing Injun Joe from harming her.

After dinner, the widow sprang a surprise of her own. She said that she meant to give Huck a home under her roof and have him educated; and that when she could spare the money, she would help him start a small business. Then Tom spoke up:

"Huck don't need it. Huck's rich."

The crowd could hardly keep from laughing at the thought that Huck Finn was rich. Knowing how strange he must have sounded, Tom continued:

"Huck's got money. Maybe you don't believe it, but he's got lots of it. Oh you needn't smile—I reckon I can show you. Just wait a minute."

Tom ran out of the door, as the guests looked more and more puzzled.

A minute later, he was back, struggling with the weight of his money sacks. He poured the mass of yellow coins out onto the table and said:

"Here—what did I tell you? Half of it's Huck's and half of it's mine!"

Nobody spoke for a moment. Then everyone began shouting for an explanation, which Tom was quick to provide. After he had finished, the money was counted—it added up to a little over twelve thousand dollars. Huck Finn *was* rich!

The Widow Douglas put Huck's money in the bank, and Aunt Polly did the same with Tom's.

As for Becky's father, Judge Thatcher now had

a great opinion of Tom. He said that no ordinary boy would have gotten his daughter out of that cave, and that he hoped to see Tom become a great lawyer or a great soldier someday. He would even see to it that Tom went to West Point and was later trained at the best law school in the entire country.

Huck Finn's wealth, and the fact that he was now under the Widow Douglas's protection, introduced him to society—no, dragged him into it—and his sufferings were almost more than he could bear. The widow's servants kept him neat and clean, combed and brushed at all times. He had to eat with a knife and fork; he had to use a napkin, cup, and plate; he had to learn his book; he had to go to church; he had to talk properly as well.

Huck bravely bore these miseries for three whole weeks until one Saturday he turned up missing. For two full days, the widow hunted for him everywhere, but no one could find the boy. Early on the third morning, Tom Sawyer went poking among some old empty hog stalls behind the abandoned grain silo and, in one of them, he found his friend. Huck had slept there that night. When Tom found him, Huck had just finished eating some stolen odds and ends of food and was wearing his old rags and enjoying a piece of gum. Tom told him about the trouble he was causing and urged him to go home.

"Don't talk about it, Tom," Huck sighed. "I've tried it, and it don't work. It ain't for me. The widow's good to me, and friendly, but I can't stand them ways. She makes me git up just at the same time every morning; she makes me wash; they comb me all to thunder; she won't let me sleep in the woodshed. I got to wear them blamed clothes that just smothers me. I got to go to church and sweat and sweat—I hate them loud sermons!"

"Well, everybody does that way, Huck."

"Tom, it makes no difference. I ain't every-body, and I can't *stand* it. Looky-here, Tom, being rich ain't what it's cracked up to be. It's just worry and worry, and sweat and sweat, and wishing you was dead all the time. You take my share of it, Tom, and gimme ten cents sometimes when I need it—and you go home and apologize for me with the widow."

"Oh, Huck, you know I can't do that. If you'll try this thing just a while longer, you'll come to like it."

"No, Tom, I won't be rich. I like the woods, and the river, and all. I'll stick to 'em, too. Dang it! Just as we was all fixed up to be robbers, this darn fool-ishness has got to come along and spoil it all!"

Tom saw his chance:

"Looky-here, Huck, being rich ain't going to keep me back from turning robber."

"Are you in real deadwood earnest, Tom?"

"Just as dead earnest as I'm sitting here. But Huck, we can't let you into the gang if you ain't respectable, you know."

"Now, Tom," Huck said. "Ain't you always been friendly to me? You wouldn't shut me out, would you? You wouldn't do that now, *would* you, Tom?"

"Huck, I wouldn't want to—but what would people say? 'My, my, Tom Sawyer's Gang! Pretty low characters in it!' They'd mean you, Huck. You wouldn't like that, and I wouldn't, either."

Huck was silent for some time, thinking over what Tom had said.

"Well, I'll go back to the widow for a month and see if I can come to stand it if you'll let me belong to the gang, Tom."

"All right, Huck, it's a deal!"

"When do we start?"

"Oh, right off. We'll get the boys together and have the initiation tonight, maybe."

"What's that?"

"It's to swear an oath to one another, and never tell the gang's secrets, even if you're chopped all to pieces, and fight anyone who hurts one of the gang."

"That's just great, Tom. That's mighty great."

"Well, I bet it is. And all the oath swearing has got to be done at midnight, in the lonesomest, awfulest place you can find. And you've got to swear on a coffin and sign your oath with your own blood!"

"Now, that's something! Why, it's a million times better than pirating. I'll stick to the widow till I rot, Tom; and if I get to be a regular ripper of a robber, and everybody talking about it, I reckon she'll be right proud how she fixed me up."

The two boys walked off, talking about their new gang and imagining all the wonderful adventures they would have.

Questions, Questions, Questions
by Arthur Pober, Ed.D.

༄

Have you ever been around a toddler who keeps asking the question "Why?" Does your teacher call on you in class with questions from your homework? Do your parents ask you questions at the dinner table about your day? We are always surrounded by questions that need a specific response. But is it possible to have a question with no right answer?

The following questions are about the book you just read. But this is not a quiz! They are designed to help you look at the people, places, and events in the story from different angles. These questions do not have specific answers. Instead, they might make you think of the story in a completely new way.

Think carefully about each question and enjoy discovering more about this classic story.

1. Tom hates doing chores. Which of your own chores is your least favorite to do?

2. Tom explained that "to make a boy want something, all you had to do was make that something hard to get." Do you believe this is true?

3. Tom and Huck talk a lot about superstitions and spells. Do you believe in such things?

4. Tom tries all sorts of strange ways to make Becky notice him. Have you ever tried to get someone's attention in an unusual way? How did it turn out?

5. Were you surprised to find out that the boys and girls in Tom's class sat on separate sides of the

room? Would you prefer your class to be divided like this?

6. Tom daydreams of being a brave pirate on the seas. What do you dream about?

7. Where would you rather be: wandering in a graveyard after dark or exploring in a cave full of bats?

8. When Becky tears the teacher's book, Tom takes the responsibility for it. Why does he do this? Have you ever taken the punishment for something you didn't do?

9. Tom and Becky find themselves lost in a cave as their last candle burns away. What would you do in that situation? Would you be calm, or would you panic? What plan would you come up with?

10. What would you do if you found a sack of gold like Tom and Huck did?

Afterword

ᔪ

First impressions are important.

Whether we are meeting new people, going to new places, or picking up a book unknown to us, first impressions count for a lot. They can lead to warm, lasting memories or can make us shy away from any future encounters.

Can you recall your own first impressions and earliest memories of reading the classics?

Do you remember wading through pages and pages of text to prepare for an exam? Or were you the child who hid under the blanket to read with a flashlight, joining forces with Robin Hood to save Maid Marian? Do you remember only how long it took you to read a lengthy novel such as *Little Women*? Or did you become best friends with the March sisters?

Even for a gifted young reader, getting through long chapters with dense language can easily become overwhelming and can obscure the richness of the story and its characters. Reading an abridged, newly crafted version of a classic novel can be the gentle introduction a child needs to explore the characters and story line without the frustration of difficult vocabulary and complex themes.

Reading an abridged version of a classic novel gives the young reader a sense of independence and the satisfaction of finishing a "grown-up" book. And when a child is engaged with and inspired by a classic story, the tone is set for further exploration of the story's themes, characters, history, and details. As a child's reading skills advance, the desire to tackle the original, unabridged version of the story will naturally emerge.

If made accessible to young readers, these stories can become invaluable tools for understanding themselves in the context of their families and social environments. This is why the Classic Starts series includes questions that stimulate discussion regarding the impact and social relevance of the characters and stories today. These questions can foster lively conversations between children and their parents or teachers. When we look at the issues, values, and standards of past times in terms of how we live now, we can appreciate literature's classic tales in a very personal and engaging way.

Share your love of reading the classics with a young child, and introduce an imaginary world real enough to last a lifetime.

DR. ARTHUR POBER, ED.D.

Dr. Arthur Pober has spent more than twenty years in the fields of early-childhood and gifted education. He is the former principal of one of the world's oldest laboratory schools for gifted youngsters, Hunter College Elementary School, and former director of Magnet Schools for the Gifted and Talented for more than 25,000 youngsters in New York City.

Dr. Pober is a recognized authority in the areas of media and child protection and is currently the U.S. representative to the European Institute for the Media and European Advertising Standards Alliance.

Explore these wonderful stories in our
Classic Starts library.